# PACKARD TAKES FLIGHT

## A BIRD'S-EYE VIEW OF COLUMBUS, OHIO

### SUSAN SACHS LEVINE

#### ILLUSTRATIONS BY ERIN McCAULEY BURCHWELL

Published by The History Press
Charleston, SC 29403
www.historypress.net

Factbox photos by and courtesy of Susan Sachs Levine and Erin McCauley Burchwell unless othewise listed: Page 4, bottom photo courtesy of *The Columbus Dispatch*; page 11, photo by Mark Gist; page 12, courtesy of Columbus Downtown Development Corp.; page 13, top photo courtesy of OSU; page 13, bottom image courtesy of the Columbus Clippers; page 15, photo courtesy of the Columbus Museum of Art; page 16, photo courtesy of Franklin Park Conservatory; page 21, image of Stinger courtesy of the Columbus Blue Jackets; page 22, photo courtesy of the Ohio Statehouse Photo Archive; page 24, top photo courtesy of CAPA; page 26, photo courtesy of the Columbus Zoo and Aquarium. Map on page 31 courtesy of Experience Columbus.

First published 2010

Manufactured in the United States

ISBN 978.1.60949.051.5

Library of Congress CIP data applied for.

---

To my son Garrett, with whom I developed my love of reading children's picture books
and
To my daughter Ellie, thanks for all your support and never-ending encouragement!
—S.S.L.

To my husband, Jason, who patiently helps me chase my dreams.
—E.M.B.

High up on the forty-first floor of the Rhodes Tower in downtown Columbus, a peregrine falcon family nests in the gravel of a window ledge. The city spreads out below like a patchwork quilt.

The RHODES TOWER, located in the center of downtown Columbus, is named after former Ohio Governor James A. Rhodes. Governor Rhodes is Ohio's longest-serving governor and was elected to four terms in the 1960s and 1970s. The Rhodes Tower was finished in 1973 and is the tallest office building in Columbus with forty-one floors.

THE COLUMBUS DISPATCH is the leading daily newspaper in Columbus. It was first published in 1871. The historic *Dispatch* building is crowned with a large ironwork sign, a famous feature of the Columbus skyline.

"I'm telling!" Penny Peregrine shouted to her brother Packard. "Mom and Dad said not to go so close to the edge!"

"I don't care. I need to exercise my wings. Mom says I'll be flying soon!" exclaimed Packard. Packard was the oldest of three falcon chicks and was always trying to prove that he was the bravest to his siblings, Penny and Pete.

"You brag too much, Packard," said Pete. Inside, Pete couldn't wait until he could fly and explore their hometown of Columbus, the capital of Ohio.

The sun was just peeking above the *Columbus Dispatch* newspaper building when Packard strutted all the way to the edge, stretched his right wing and then his left. He turned to see if his brother and sister were impressed.

Suddenly, a gust of wind whipped by and threw Packard off balance. He felt himself falling through the air. Packard flapped his wings as hard as he could, struggling to stay aloft. He glanced up at Penny and Pete's frightened faces and then down at the street below.

A big truck stopped right under him. He lurched up, then tumbled down, landing clumsily in the truck bed—inside a large box filled with brightly colored balls.

"Oh my gosh!" gasped Packard. The truck began to move forward with a loud roar. Packard wasn't sure what was happening, but he looked up at his siblings and gave them an "OK" sign, pretending to look confident. If only he felt that way!

As the truck rattled along, Packard's heart was thumping but he tried to remain calm. Before he could think of a plan to get back to his nest, the truck stopped. Men started carrying off the boxes of balls into a huge gray building.

Once inside, a worker dumped the balls into a large bin. Packard jumped out just in time and watched in amazement as children began scrambling for the balls and tossing them up high into funnels and tubes.

As he surveyed the room, he spied a mouse. "Hi there, is this the Rhodes Tower?" asked Packard politely, trying to remember the manners his mother had taught him.

"No way—don't you know? This is COSI, the biggest, most awesome science center around!" replied the mouse.

"Wow!" said Packard. He looked around and saw kids playing with laser beams, magnets and pulleys. Close by, he watched boys and girls busy taking apart old radios and computer keyboards to see how they worked.

A loud *ka-boom!* from a nearby science show made Packard jump and head for the exit.

The CENTER OF SCIENCE AND INDUSTRY, known as COSI, was recently named the #1 Science Center by *Parents Magazine* and is located on the banks of the Scioto River near downtown Columbus. It features over three hundred interactive exhibits and an opportunity to see real science in action. Permanent exhibits explore outer space, our oceans, technology and innovation, health and history. A seven-story Extreme Screen theater, a Little Kidspace and daily science shows, including a popular rat basketball show, are all part of the fun.

When he got outside, he saw a group of children climbing aboard a big yellow bus. Packard scurried on and hid under a seat just as the bus started driving away from the science center.

When the bus stopped, Packard found himself gazing up at a huge sailing ship. A colony of ants was marching, single file, across a railing. Packard inquired, "Can you tell me the way to the Rhodes Tower?"

"I have no knowledge of that place, SIR! This is the *Santa Maria*, SIR! It is an exact replica of the Spanish ship that Christopher Columbus commanded in 1492 when he discovered America!" barked the ant with military precision. With a final salute he added, "The city of Columbus was named in his honor, SIR!"

"At ease, soldier," responded Packard as he climbed onboard. After pecking around in the galley area and sleeping quarters on deck, he looked up at the huge mast, sail and crow's nest. Packard could not resist climbing up the rope ladder.

The *SANTA MARIA* in downtown Columbus is the world's most authentic replica of Christopher Columbus's ship. At ninety-eight feet long, the ship's main mast, which holds the largest sail, is sixty-five feet tall and is made from a single Douglas fir tree. The original *Santa Maria* never left the New World. It ran aground in what is known today as the island of Haiti. Columbus had the ship taken apart and used the wood to build a fort.

The SCIOTO MILE is being constructed along the banks of the Scioto River in downtown Columbus to celebrate the city's bicentennial, or 200th birthday. The beautiful park will open June 2011 and feature walking paths along a canal, a bikeway, a band shell, a large fountain and a café. Various festivals and events will be held at this great venue every summer.

At the top, he looked down over a glassy, blue-gray river. To the north, Packard could see a diamond-shaped field and, farther on, a horseshoe-shaped stadium. To the south was a beautiful park with a giant fountain.

Oh, how his heart ached suddenly! The river reminded him of his mother. She would leave the nest every day to clean her feathers in the Scioto River. This must be the place, but to Packard's disappointment, she was nowhere to be seen.

Trying to muster his courage, he got off the ship and jumped into a police car while the officer was not looking. *Perhaps he is going to the Rhodes Tower,* thought Packard.

OHIO STADIUM, also known as "The Horseshoe" because of its shape, is home to The Ohio State University football team. The team is nicknamed the "Buckeyes" after the state tree of Ohio. More than 110,000 fans pack the stadium every fall to cheer their team on to victory. The Ohio State University is located just four miles north of downtown and is the leading teaching and research institution in the state with more than 52,000 students.

HUNTINGTON PARK is the home of the Columbus Clippers, a Triple-A baseball team affiliated with the Cleveland Indians. Its innovative, fan-friendly design earned it the distinction of being voted "Baseball Park of the Year" in 2009 by Baseballparks.com. Located in Columbus's Arena District, the city's newest entertainment area, Huntington Park is an easy walk from popular hotels, restaurants and nightlife.

He found himself at the entrance to a tree-filled courtyard. A squirrel sat in the middle of a curious-looking tea party, nibbling a nut. "Can you tell me if this is the Rhodes Tower?" asked Packard.

"*Non, non Monsieur*, you are mistaken. This is the Columbus Museum of Art, home to masterpieces from around the world. *Entre, s'il vous plait*, and your senses will be awakened," beckoned the squirrel in perfect French.

*Well, that might cheer me up*, thought Packard.

Inside, Packard entered a big room with magnificent paintings! His favorite was a woman with a big red hat and a face as emerald green as the leaves on the trees below his nest. *Oh, my nest*, thought Packard sadly.

The Columbus Museum of Art is located on Broad Street in downtown Columbus and is in the midst of a multimillion-dollar renovation and expansion. Inside, you can see paintings by many famous artists, including Picasso, Degas and Matisse. The museum also has a Center for Creativity where families can explore art together, an outdoor sculpture garden featuring an innovative Alice in Wonderland chess set by local artist Joan Vobst and a delicious café.

The FRANKLIN PARK CONSERVATORY is located just two miles east of downtown Columbus. Inside, you can explore four separate greenhouses that have plants and animals from different climates around the world: the Himalayan Mountains, a tropical rainforest, a dry desert and a Pacific island water garden. The conservatory owns many pieces of glass by famed artist Dale Chihuly that it exhibits from time to time. Every spring and summer, the Pacific Garden has a special exhibit of live butterflies.

In front of the museum, a family was climbing into a taxicab. Packard sneaked inside, sure they would be going to the Rhodes Tower. Instead, they arrived at a big building with a glass roof. Inside was a beautiful jungle of plants, trees and flowers.

He saw a sign that read "Franklin Park Conservatory." *A conservatory—awesome!* thought Packard.

Moments later, Packard entered a magical room with butterflies, a waterfall and giant goldfish swimming in a pond. In the middle of the room was the most magnificent tower of orange glass Packard had ever seen.

A plate of fruit, where several butterflies were eating, caught his eye and made him realize that he was getting very hungry. He must find his way home!

Outside, a city bus pulled up and Packard flapped his way on, hiding under the big skirt of a woman next to him. Hoping the bus was going to the Rhodes Tower, he crossed his wing tips for good luck!

They were heading toward the tall buildings of downtown—Packard was hopeful! They passed a beautiful park that had figures of people made out of velvet green bushes.

*That looks like a fun place to play if I ever get out of this mess,* Packard thought to himself.

The TOPIARY PARK is located in downtown Columbus around the corner from the Columbus Metropolitan Main Library. In this pretty setting, George Seurat's famous post-Impressionist painting, *A Sunday on the Island of La Grande Jatte*, is created in topiary or shaped bushes. The display is situated around a pond that represents the Seine River in Paris and has fifty-four topiary people, eight boats, three dogs, a monkey and a cat.

The bus stopped in front of a building that had a big rooster on the outside. A black and tan beagle was tied to a post. "Excuse me, but do you know the way to the Rhodes Tower?" asked Packard, for what seemed like the hundredth time.

"What's it smell like?" asked the beagle. "I can sniff out a rabbit a mile away." Seeing Packard's disappointed face he added, "This is the North Market—go on in, there's food galore!"

*I'm starving!* thought Packard as he dashed inside.

There were dozens of shopkeepers selling meat, fruits, vegetables and flowers. Then he saw something that truly amazed him. At the poultry stand, all the birds were just lying there, and they already had their feathers plucked! Packard was sure he could catch one.

*Mom will be so proud of me when I bring home one of these big birds,* thought Packard. However, when Packard lunged to grab one, his head banged into an invisible wall! "Ouch!" he yelled. A little dizzy, Packard staggered toward the door. A snack would have to wait.

Out on the sidewalk there was a sea of people. They were racing toward a big building talking excitedly about shots on goal and hat tricks.

Packard was about to follow when he spied a long, black car. The license plate read "GOVERNOR."Packard knew that the Rhodes Tower was named after James Rhodes, a former governor of Ohio. Sure that this car would take him home, Packard quickly ducked inside.

The National Hockey League's COLUMBUS BLUE JACKETS bring the excitement of professional hockey to the city every season. The Jackets play at NATIONWIDE ARENA, one of the premier entertainment complexes in the country, located in the heart of Columbus's Arena District. Stinger, the team mascot, buzzes around the games entertaining the crowd with his antics. He loves a Blue Jacket's "hat trick," when the same player scores three goals in a single game and the fans throw their hats onto the ice in celebration. Besides the Jackets, Nationwide hosts a wide variety of world-class concerts and shows.

The OHIO STATEHOUSE is one of our country's best examples of Greek Revival architecture. Finished in 1861, it is one of the oldest statehouses in the United States still in use. The main feature of the statehouse is the rotunda, or high domed ceiling in the center. A stained-glass Seal of Ohio is in the middle. Today, the governor of Ohio has his office in the Statehouse. The Ohio House of Representatives, with ninety-nine members, and the Ohio Senate, with thirty-three members, also meet in the Statehouse.

When the car came to a stop, Packard recognized the huge, white building with the cupola on top. This was the Statehouse, the center of government for Ohio. He was close!

"Mom, I'm here!" he called out, as he scrambled up the steps. *If I can just get to the top*, Packard thought, *I'll be able to see my nest*.

Up one flight of steps, Packard found the House of Representatives Chamber. Lots of men and women dressed in suits were sitting behind wooden desks and pushing a button to vote.

Nearby was the Senate Chamber. There were not as many people in this room. They were listening to a person talk about a new law to protect endangered birds.

The OHIO THEATRE and Trinity Episcopal Church are located on Capitol Square in downtown Columbus. Both are listed on the National Register of Historic Places. The Ohio Theatre began as a movie palace in 1928 and featured its own orchestra. Today it is used by a variety of performing arts groups, including the Columbus Symphony Orchestra and BalletMet.

The TRINITY EPISCOPAL CHURCH was built in 1869 and features beautiful stained-glass windows, a large pipe organ and a bell tower.

Finally Packard made it to the top of the building. He squeezed out a partially opened window into the fresh air. Looking one way he saw the Ohio Theatre.

Another way, he saw the Trinity Church. He remembered hearing the bells in the tower ring every hour from his nest. Then finally, there it was—the Rhodes Tower! And perched on the window ledge of the forty-first floor was his nest. "Yahoo!" he cried.

Packard started flapping his wings, calling, "Mom, it's me! Over here, Packard!"

All of a sudden, he looked down and realized that he was no longer standing on the windowsill, but he wasn't falling either. He was flying!

With all his energy, Packard flapped his wings wildly and started to make his way toward the Rhodes Tower and his family.

*Just a little farther...*

The COLUMBUS ZOO AND AQUARIUM, home of Jungle Jack Hanna, is located ten miles north of the city. Voted the #1 Zoo in America by *USA Travel Guide* in 2009, the Columbus Zoo features Asian elephants, Amur tigers, West Indian manatees and polar bears in state-of-the-art natural enclosures. Zoombezi Bay, a twenty-two-acre water park, is attached to the zoo and offers fifteen water slides, a wave pool and a lazy river for those hot Columbus summer days!

His mother and father could not believe their eyes. They jumped and whistled in circles around him, so elated that he was home.

"You've taught yourself to fly, you clever boy!" exclaimed his mother.

"What a wonderful surprise!" said his father. "First thing tomorrow morning, I am going to take you out and show you all the sights of Columbus—COSI, the Art Museum, the North Market and the Columbus Zoo! Elephants, gorillas, lions, polar bears...even a water park."

But Packard wasn't listening; he was so tired from his journey that he had fallen asleep and was already dreaming about his next big adventure!

# Author's Note

Peregrine falcons were first introduced into downtown Columbus in 1989 as part of the Peregrine Falcon Restoration Project. Other cities in Ohio, such as Akron, Dayton and Cincinnati, participated as well, releasing juvenile falcons each spring until 1992. The falcons were banded so that they could be tracked and monitored. Peregrine falcon numbers had plummeted in the 1960s due to the use of pesticides like DDT. The forty-first floor of the Rhodes Tower was selected as the site to build a nesting platform because the skyscraper could simulate the southern exposure cliffs that the peregrines prefer.

Aurora feeding her chicks. *Photo by Tim Daniel, Ohio Department of Natural Resources.*

In 1994, Columbus had its first successful nest at the Rhodes Tower. The female, Aurora, was a falcon that had been released in Ontario, Canada, as part of the recovery program, while the male, Bandit, was wild. They produced nineteen chicks during five seasons of nesting. Several of their offspring have gone on to establish territories of their own, successfully producing young to further the species.

In the spring of 2009, the Rhodes Tower nesting territory was occupied by a male named Orville and a female, Scout. Orville was a falcon that hatched in Dayton in 2003 and was named for Orville Wright, the great Ohio aviation inventor who hails from that area. Scout hatched in Detroit, Michigan, in 2004. They nested for the first time in 2007, but no chicks were produced. Their luck changed in 2008 when a full brood of four healthy chicks hatched and fledged—Boomer, Justice, Mistic and Columbus. Another three female chicks were successfully raised in 2009—Aerial, Jet and Eclipse. Unfortunately, in the summer of 2009, Orville was found dead on a street on the outskirts of downtown, apparently the result of a collision, perhaps with a car.

Sightings of Scout around the nesting platform continued all summer and fall of 2009. While some peregrines migrate to warmer climates in the winter, the Rhodes Tower falcons, including Scout, have been content to stay in Columbus, apparently finding plenty of warmth and food. With the onset of the 2010 mating season, a new male that was migrating through Columbus discovered Scout and her attractive accommodations at the Rhodes Tower. Given the name Trooper, he took up residence in March, and by late May, Scout and Trooper were the proud parents of two downy white chicks. This appears to be a good sign that Columbus will continue its successful track record of peregrine falcons nesting above our beautiful city.

In Columbus, the ODNR Division of Wildlife monitors the falcon nest at the Rhodes Tower via live streaming video and audio. You can view this video and get updates on the birds' activities by going to www.wildohio.com and clicking on "Experience Wildlife."

## Learn More About Peregrine Falcons

The peregrine falcon, historically known as the "Duck Hawk," is a large falcon about the size of a crow. Its habitat ranges all the way from the Arctic Tundra to the Tropics, making it the world's most widespread falcon. The adult peregrine is a handsome bird with a blue-gray back and head and a "mustache." The under parts are barred white. As with other birds of prey, the female is significantly bigger than the male.

Peregrine falcons return to the same nesting spot year after year. They do not bring any materials to build a nest; they simply make a depression in the dirt or gravel of the nesting ledge. In North America, mating behavior can usually be seen beginning in late January and February, and by March or April three to four eggs will be laid. The eggs are slightly smaller than a chicken egg.

The male and female take turns incubating the eggs. When the chicks hatch, they are covered in a creamy-white down. The chicks fledge, or learn to fly, about forty-five days after hatching, replacing their white fluff with the sleek brown flying feathers of a juvenile. They remain dependent on their parents for food for as long as two months.

Peregrine falcons hunt during daylight hours, feeding primarily on birds ranging in size from a sparrow to a duck. Once the peregrine spots its prey, it can dive at speeds up to two hundred miles per hour, striking and capturing the prey with its talons in midair. In urban areas, feral pigeons are a common prey, along with starlings, mourning doves and even songbirds. The male does the majority of the hunting for the female and young chicks. The adults will generally pluck the prey for the young before they eat.

Peregrine falcons keep the same mate from year to year, but if one of the pair is injured or killed, the other will quickly seek a new mate. On average, peregrines have a lengthy lifespan of twelve to fifteen years in the wild.

Due to successful breeding and introduction programs, peregrine falcons were removed from the Federal Endangered Species List in 1999. The species was downgraded to "threatened" in Ohio in 2009.

## Why Packard?

When picking a name for the main character in my book, I wanted a name that had a connection to Ohio. I chose Packard to honor the Packard family of Warren, Ohio, who established the Packard Electric Company in 1890, making durable electric cable. The family later went on to found the Packard Motor Car Company in 1902.

The family's two interests merged when the electrical side of the business started designing improved electrical systems for motorcars. Today, the Delphi Packard Electrical/Electronic Architecture Company is recognized globally for its excellence in automotive wiring and components for today's sophisticated vehicles.

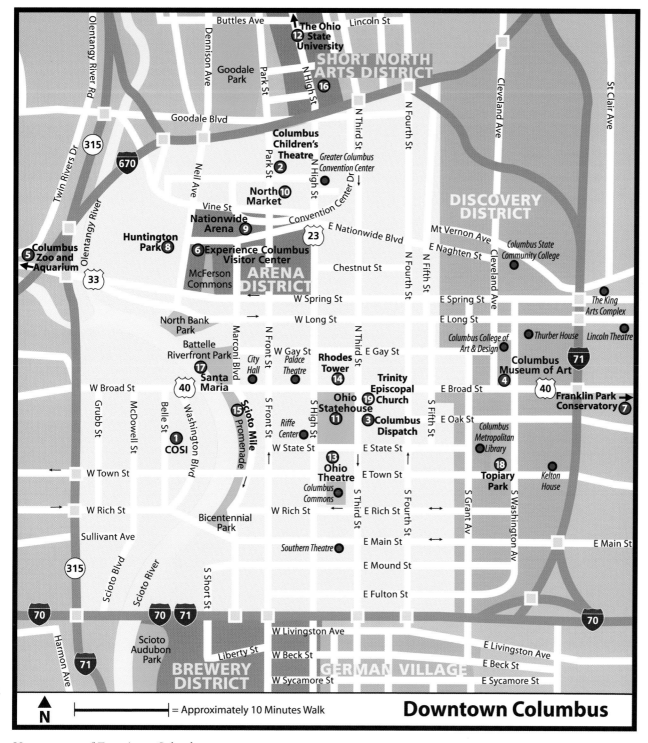

Buttles Ave
Lincoln St

**The Ohio State University** 12

SHORT NORTH ARTS DISTRICT

16

Olentangy River Rd
Dennison Ave
Goodale Park
Park St
N High St
N Third St
N Fourth St
Cleveland Ave
St Clair Ave

Goodale Blvd

315
670

**Columbus Children's Theatre** 2
Greater Columbus Convention Center

**North Market** 10

DISCOVERY DISTRICT

Convention Center Dr
E Nationwide Blvd

Twin Rivers Dr
Olentangy River
Neil Ave
Vine St
**Nationwide Arena** 9
23
Mt Vernon Ave
E Naghten St
**Columbus State Community College**

**Huntington Park** 8
**Experience Columbus Visitor Center** 6
Chestnut St
N Fourth St
N Fifth St
Cleveland Ave

5 **Columbus Zoo and Aquarium**
McFerson Commons
ARENA DISTRICT
W Spring St
E Spring St
**The King Arts Complex**

33

North Bank Park
W Long St
E Long St
**Thurber House**
**Lincoln Theatre**

Battelle Riverfront Park
Marconi Blvd
N Front St
W Gay St
N Third St
E Gay St
**Columbus College of Art & Design**

17
City Hall
Palace Theatre
**Rhodes Tower** 14
71
**Columbus Museum of Art** 4

W Broad St
40
**Santa Maria**
Scioto Mile Promenade
**Trinity Episcopal Church** 19
**Ohio Statehouse** 11
E Broad St
40
**Franklin Park Conservatory** 7

Grubb St
McDowell St
Washington Blvd
Belle St
15
Riffe Center
S Front St
S High St
3 **Columbus Dispatch**
S Fifth St
E Oak St
**Columbus Metropolitan Library**
S Washington Av

1 **COSI**
W State St
E State St
**Topiary Park** 18
**Kelton House**

W Town St
**Ohio Theatre** 13
E Town St

W Rich St
Columbus Commons
W Rich St
S Third St
E Rich St
S Fourth St
S Grant Av

Bicentennial Park
E Main St
E Main St

Sullivant Ave
**Southern Theatre**
E Mound St

315
E Fulton St

Scioto Blvd
Scioto River
S Short St

70
70 71
W Livingston Ave
E Livingston Ave
70

Harmon Ave
71
Scioto Audubon Park
Liberty St
W Beck St
W Sycamore St
E Beck St
E Sycamore St

BREWERY DISTRICT
GERMAN VILLAGE

▲ N
|———| = Approximately 10 Minutes Walk
**Downtown Columbus**

You may wish to visit many of the wonderful Columbus sites mentioned in this book. To help plan your tour, use this map and the contact information that follows.

Enjoy!

Map courtesy of Experience Columbus.

1. Center of Science and Industry (COSI)
333 West Broad Street
Columbus, Ohio 43215
888-819-2674
614-228-2674
www.cosi.org

2. Columbus Children's Theatre
512 Park Street
Columbus, Ohio 43215
614-224-6672
www.colschildrenstheatre.org

3. *The Columbus Dispatch*
34 South Third Street
Columbus, Ohio 43215
614-461-5000
www.dispatch.com

4. Columbus Museum of Art
480 East Broad Street
Columbus, Ohio 43215
614-221-6801
www.columbusmuseum.org

5. Columbus Zoo and Aquarium
4850 West Powell Road
Powell, Ohio 43065
614-645-3550
www.columbuszoo.org

6. Experience Columbus
(Convention & Visitors Bureau)
277 W. Nationwide Boulevard, Suite 125
Columbus, Ohio 43215
614-221-6623
www.ExperienceColumbus.com

7. Franklin Park Conservatory
1777 East Broad Street
Columbus, Ohio 43203
800-214-7275
www.fpconservatory.org

8. Huntington Park
Home of the Columbus Clippers
330 Huntington Park Lane
Columbus, Ohio 43215
For tickets: 614-462-2757
www.clippersbaseball.com

9. Nationwide Arena
Home of the Columbus Blue Jackets
200 W. Nationwide Boulevard
Columbus, Ohio 43215
For tickets: 1-800-645-2657
www.nationwidearena.com
www.bluejackets.com

10. North Market
59 Spruce Street
Columbus, Ohio 43215
614-463-9664
www.northmarket.com

11. Ohio Statehouse
1 Capitol Square
Columbus, Ohio 43215
888-OHIO-123
www.ohiostatehouse.org

12. Ohio Stadium, The Ohio State University
411 Woody Hayes Drive
Columbus, Ohio 43210
614-292-6446
www.ohiostatebuckeyes.com

13. Ohio Theatre
BalletMet, the Columbus Symphony
Orchestra and more
55 East State Street
Columbus, Ohio 43215
614-469-0939
www.capa.com/columbus/venues/ohio
www.columbussymphony.com
www.balletmet.org

14. Rhodes State Office Tower
30 East Broad Street
Columbus, Ohio 43215
614-466-7361
www.oba.ohio.gov

15. Scioto Mile
Civic Center Drive between Broad Street
and Main Street
Columbus, Ohio 43215
www.sciotomile.com

16. Short North Business Association
1126½A North High Street
Columbus, Ohio 43201
614-299-8050
www.shortnorth.org

17. *Santa Maria*
25 Marconi Boulevard
Columbus, Ohio 43215
614-645-8760
www.santamaria.org

18. Topiary Park
480 East Town Street
Columbus, Ohio 43215
614-645-0197
www.topiarygarden.org

19. Trinity Episcopal Church
125 East Broad Street
Columbus, Ohio 43215
614-221-5351
www.trinitycolumbus.org